THE BOWMEN

AND OTHER SHORT STORIES BY ARTHUR MACHEN

British Library Cataloguing-in-Publication Data
A catalogue record for this book is available from
the British Library

Contents

OUT OF THE EARTH

*   *   *

There was some sort of confused complaint during last

August of the ill behaviour of the children at certain Welsh watering places. Such reports and vague rumours are most difficult to trace to their heads and fountains; none has better reason to know that than myself. I need not go over the old ground here, but I am afraid that many people are wishing by this time that they had never heard my name; again, a considerable number of estimable persons are concerning themselves gloomily enough, from my point of view, with my everlasting welfare. They write me letters, some in kindly remonstrance, begging me not to deprive poor, sick-hearted souls of what little comfort they possess amidst their sorrows. Others send me tracts and pink leaflets with allusions to 'the daughter of a well-known canon'; others again are violently and anonymously abusive. And then in open print, in fair book form, Mr. Begbie has dealt with me righteously but harshly, as I cannot but think.

Yet, it was all so entirely innocent, nay casual, on my part. A poor linnet of prose, I did but perform my indifferent piping in the *Evening News* because I wanted to do so, because I felt that the story of 'The Bowmen' ought to be told. An inventor of fantasies is a poor creature, heaven knows, when all the world is at war; but I thought that no harm would be done, at any rate, if I bore witness, after the fashion of the fantastic craft, to my belief in the heroic glory of the English host who went back from Mons fighting and triumphing.

And then, somehow or other, it was as if I had touched a button and set in action a terrific, complicated mechanism of rumours that pretended to be sworn truth, of gossip that posed as evidence, of wild tarradiddles that good men most firmly believed. The supposed testimony of that 'daughter of a well-known canon' took parish magazines by storm, and equally enjoyed the faith of dissenting divines. The 'daughter' denied all knowledge of the matter, but people still quoted her supposed sure word; and the issues were confused with tales, probably true, of painful hallucinations and deliriums of our retreating soldiers, men fatigued and shattered to the very verge of death. It all became worse than the Russian myths, and as in the fable of the Russians, it seemed impossible to follow the streams of delusion to their fountain-head – or heads, who was it who said that 'Miss M knew two officers who, etc., etc.'? I suppose we shall never know his lying, deluding name.

And so, I dare say, it will be with this strange affair of the troublesome children of the Welsh seaside town, or rather of a group of small towns and villages lying within a certain section or zone, which I am not going to indicate more precisely than I can help, since I love that country, and my recent experiences with 'The Bowmen' have taught me that no tale is too idle to be believed. And, of course, to begin with, nobody knew how this odd and malicious piece of gossip originated. So far as I know, it was more akin to the Russian myth than to the tale of 'The Angels of Mons'. That is, rumour preceded print; the thing was talked of here and there and passed from letter to letter long before the papers were aware of its existence. And – here it resembles rather the Mons affair – London and Manchester, Leeds and Birmingham were muttering vague unpleasant things while the little villages concerned basked innocently in the sunshine of an unusual prosperity.

In this last circumstance, as some believe, is to be sought the root of the whole matter. It is well known that certain east coast towns suffered from the dread of air-raids, and that a good many of their usual visitors went westward for the first time. So there is a theory that the east coast was mean enough to circulate reports against the west coast out of pure malice and envy. It may be so; I do not pretend to know. But here is a personal experience, such as it is, which illustrated the way in which the rumour was circulated. I was lunching one day at my Fleet Street tavern – this was early in July – and a friend of mine, a solicitor, of Serjeants' Inn, came in and sat at the same table. We began to talk of holidays and my friend Eddis asked me where I was going. 'To the same old place,' I said. 'Manavon. You know we always go there.' 'Are you really?' said the lawyer; 'I thought that coast had gone off a lot. My wife has a friend who's heard that it's not at all what it was.'

I was astonished to hear this, not seeing how a little village like Manavon could have 'gone off'. I had known it for ten years as having accommodation for about twenty visitors, and I could not believe that rows of lodging houses had sprung up since the August of 1914. Still I put the question to Eddis: 'Trippers?' I asked, knowing firstly that trippers hate the solitudes of the country and the sea; secondly, that there are no industrial towns within cheap and easy distance, and thirdly, that the railways were issuing no excursion tickets during the war.

'No, not exactly trippers,' the lawyer replied. 'But my wife's friend knows a clergyman who says that the beach at Tremaen is not at all pleasant now, and Tremaen's only a few miles from Manavon, isn't it?'

'In what way not pleasant?' I carried on my examination. 'Pierrots and shows, and that sort of thing?' I felt that it could not be so, for the solemn rocks of Tremaen would have turned the liveliest Pierrot to stone. He would have frozen into a crag on the beach, and the seagulls would carry away his song and make it a lament by lonely, booming caverns that look on Avalon. Eddis said he had heard nothing about showmen, but he understood that since the war the children of the whole district had gone quite out of hand.

'Bad language, you know,' he said, 'and all that sort of thing, worse than London slum children. One doesn't want one's wife and children to hear foul talk at any time, much less on their holiday. And they say that Castell Coch is quite impossible; no decent woman would be seen there!'

I said: 'Really, that's a great pity,' and changed the subject. But I could not make it out at all. I knew Castell Coch well – a little bay bastioned by dunes and red sandstone cliffs, rich with greenery. A stream of cold water runs down there to the sea; there is the ruined Norman Castle, the ancient church and the scattered village; it is altogether a place of peace and quiet and great beauty. The people there, chil-

T-B

dren and grown-ups alike, were not merely decent but courteous folk: if one thanked a child for opening a gate, there would come the inevitable response: 'And welcome kindly, sir.' I could not make it out at all. I didn't believe the lawyer's tales; for the life of me I could not see what he could be driving at. And, for the avoidance of all unnecessary mystery, I may as well say that my wife and child and myself went down to Manavon last August and had a most delightful holiday. At the time we were certainly conscious of no annoyance or unpleasantness of any kind. Afterwards, I confess, I heard a story that puzzled and still puzzles me, and this story, if it be received, might give its own interpretation to one or two circumstances which seemed in themselves quite insignificant.

But all through July I came upon traces of evil rumours affecting this most gracious corner of the earth. Some of these rumours were repetitions of Eddis's gossip; others amplified his vague story and made it more definite. Of course, no first-hand evidence was available. There never is any first-hand evidence in these cases. But A knew B who had heard from C that her second cousin's little girl had been set upon and beaten by a pack of young Welsh savages. Then people quoted 'a doctor in large practice in a well-known town in the Midlands', to the effect that Tremaen was a sink of juvenile depravity. They said that a responsible medical man's evidence was final and convincing; but they didn't bother to find out who the doctor was, or whether there was any doctor at all – or any doctor relevant to the issue. Then the thing began to get into the papers in a sort of oblique, by-the-way sort of manner. People cited the case of these imaginary bad children in support of their educational views. One side said that 'these unfortunate little ones' would have been quite well behaved if they had no education at all; the opposition declared that continuation schools would speedily reform them and make them into admirable citizens. Then the poor Arfonshire children seemed to become involved in quarrels about Welsh disestablishment and in the question of the miners; and all the while they were going about behaving politely and admirably as they always do behave. I knew all the time that it was all nonsense, but I couldn't understand in the least what it meant, or who was pulling the wires of rumour, or their purpose in so pulling. I began to wonder whether the pressure and anxiety and suspense of a terrible war had unhinged the public mind, so that it was ready to believe any fable, to debate the reasons for happenings which had never happened. At last, quite incredible things began to be whispered: visitors' children had not only been beaten, they had been tortured; a little boy had been found impaled on a stake in a lonely field near Manavon; another child had been lured to destruction over the cliffs at Castell Coch. A London paper sent a good man down quietly to Arfon to investigate. He was away for a week, and at the end of that period returned to his office and in his own phrase, 'threw the whole story down'. There was not a word of truth, he said, in any of these rumours, no vestige of a foundation for the mildest forms of all this gossip. He had never seen such a beautiful country; he had never met pleasanter men, women or children; there was not a single case of anyone having been annoyed or troubled in any sort of fashion.

Yet all the while the story grew, and grew more monstrous and incredible. I was too much occupied in watching the progress of my own mythological monster to pay much attention. The town clerk of Tremaen, to which the legend had at length penetrated, wrote a brief letter to the press indignantly denying that there was the slightest foundation for 'the unsavoury rumours' which, he understood, were being circulated; and about this time we went down to Manavon and, as I say, enjoyed ourselves extremely. The weather was perfect: blues of paradise in the skies, the seas all a shimmering wonder, olive greens and emeralds, rich purples, glassy sapphires changing by the rocks; far away a haze of magic lights and colours at the meeting of sea and sky. Work and anxiety had harried me; I found nothing better than to rest on the thymy banks by the shore, finding an infinite balm and refreshment in the great sea before me, in the tiny flowers beside me. Or we would rest all the summer afternoon on a 'shelf' high on the grey cliffs and watch the tide creaming and surging about the rocks, and listen to it booming in the hollows and caverns below. Afterwards, as I say, there were one or two things that struck cold. But at the time those were nothing. You see a man in an odd white hat pass by and think little or nothing about it. Afterwards, when you hear that a man wearing just such a hat had committed murder in the next street five minutes before, then you find in that hat a certain interest and significance. 'Funny children,' was the phrase my little boy used; and I began to think they were 'funny' indeed.

If there be a key at all to this queer business, I think it is to be found in a talk I had not long ago with a friend of mine named Morgan. He is a Welshman and a dreamer, and some people say he is like a child who has grown up and yet has not grown up like other children of men. Though I did not know it, while I was at Manavon, he was spending his holiday time at Castell Coch. He was a lonely man and he liked lonely places, and when we met in the autumn he told me how, day after day, he would carry his bread and cheese and beer in a basket to a remote headland on that coast known as the Old Camp. Here, far above the waters, are solemn, mighty walls, turf-grown; circumvallations rounded and smooth with the passing of many thousand years. At one end of this most ancient place there is a tumulus, a tower of observation, perhaps, and underneath it slinks the green, deceiving ditch that seems to wind into the heart of the camp, but in reality rushes down to sheer rock and a precipice over the waters.

Here came Morgan daily, as he said, to dream of Avalon, to purge himself from the fuming corruption of the streets.

And so, as he told me, it was with singular horror that one afternoon as he dozed and dreamed and opened his eyes now and again to watch the miracle and magic of the sea, as he listened to the myriad murmurs of the waves, his meditation was broken by a sudden burst of horrible raucous cries – and the cries of children, too, but children of the lowest type.

Morgan says that the very tones made him shudder – 'They were to the ear what slime is to the touch,' and then the words: every foulness, every filthy abomination of speech; blasphemies that struck like blows at the sky, that sank down into the pure, shining depths, defiling them! He was amazed. He peered over the green wall of the fort, and there in the ditch he saw a swarm of noisome children, horrible little stunted creatures with old men's faces, with bloated faces, with little sunken eyes, with leering eyes. It was worse than uncovering a brood of snakes or a nest of worms.

No; he would not describe what they were about. 'Read about Belgium,' said Morgan, 'and think they couldn't have been more than five or six years old.' There was no infamy, he said, that they did not perpetrate; they spared no horror of cruelty. 'I saw blood running in streams, as they shrieked with laughter, but I could not find the mark of it on the grass afterwards.'

Morgan said he watched them and could not utter a word; it was as if a hand held his mouth tight. But at last he found his voice and shrieked at them, and they burst into a yell of obscene laughter and shrieked back at him, and scattered out of sight. He could not trace them; he supposes that they hid in the deep bracken behind the Old Camp.

'Sometimes I can't understand my landlord at Castell Coch,' Morgan went on. 'He's the village postmaster and has a little farm of his own – a decent, pleasant, ordinary sort of chap. But now and again he will talk oddly. I was telling him about these beastly children and wondering who they could be when he broke into Welsh, something like "the battle that is for age unto ages; and the People take delight in it".'

So far Morgan, and it was evident that he did not understand at all. But this strange tale of his brought back an odd circumstance or two that I recollected: a matter of our little boy straying away more than once, and getting lost among the sand dunes and coming back screaming, evidently frightened horribly, and babbling about 'funny children'. We took no notice; did not trouble, I think, to look whether there were any children wandering about the dunes or not. We were accustomed to his small imaginations.

But after hearing Morgan's story I was interested and I wrote an account of the matter to my friend, old Doctor Duthoit, of Hereford. And he replied:

'They were only visible, only audible to children and the child-like. Hence the explanation of what puzzled you at first; the rumours, how did they arise? They arose from nursery gossip, from scraps and odds and ends of half-articulate children's talk of horrors that they didn't understand, of words that shamed their nurses and their mothers.

'These little people of the earth rise up and rejoice in these times of ours. For they are glad, as the Welshman said, when they know that men follow their ways.'

The Cosy Room

And he found to his astonishment that he came to the appointed place with a sense of profound relief. It was true that the window was somewhat high up in the wall and that, in case of fire, it might be difficult, for many reasons to get out that way; it was barred like the basement windows that one sees now and then in London houses, but as for the rest it was an extremely snug room.

There was a gay flowering paper on the walls, a hanging bookshelf – his stomach sickened for an instant – a little table under the window with a board and checkers on it, two or three good pictures, religious and ordinary, and the man who looked after him was arranging the tea-things on the table in the middle of the room. And there was a nice wicker chair by a bright fire.

It was a thoroughly pleasant room; snug you would call it.

And, thank God, it was all over, anyhow . . .

It had been a horrible time for the last three months, up to an hour ago. First of all, there was the trouble; all over in a minute, that was, and couldn't be helped, though it was a pity, and the girl wasn't worth it. But then there was the getting out of the town.

He thought at first of just going about his ordinary business and knowing nothing about it; he didn't think that anybody had seen him following Joe down to the river. Why not loaf about as usual, and say nothing, and go into the Ringland Arms for a pint?

It might be days before they found the body under the alders; and there would be an inquest, and all that. Would it be the best plan just to stick it out, and hold his tongue if the police came asking him questions?

But then, how could he account for himself and his doings that evening? He might say he went for a stroll in Bleadon Woods and home again without meeting anybody. There was nobody who could contradict him that he could think of.

And now, sitting in the snug room with the bright wallpaper, sitting in the cosy chair by the fire – all so different from the tales they told of such places – he wished he had stuck it out and faced it out, and let them come on and find out what they could.

But, then, he had got frightened. Lots of men had heard him swearing it would be 'outing dos' for Joe if he didn't leave the girl alone. And he had shown his revolver to Dick Haddon, and 'Lobster' Carey, and Finniman, and others, and then they would be fitting the bullet into the revolver, and it would be all up.

He got into a panic and shook with terror, and knew he could never stay in Ledham, not another hour.

Mrs Evans, his landlady, was spending the evening with her married sister at the other side of the town, and would not be back till eleven. He shaved off his stubbly black beard and moustache, and slunk out of town in the dark and walked all through the night by a lonely byroad, and got to Darnley, twenty miles away, in the morning in time to catch the London excursion.

There was a great crowd of people, and so far as he could see, nobody that he knew, and the carriages packed full of Darnleyites and Lockwood weavers all in high spirits and taking no notice of him. They all got out at Kings Cross, and he strolled about with the rest, and looked round here and there as they did and had a glass of beer at a crowded bar. He didn't see how anybody was to find out where he had gone.

He got a back room in a quiet street off the Caledonian Road, and waited. There was something in the evening paper that night, something that you couldn't very well make out. By the next day Joe's body was found, and they got to Murder – the doctor said it couldn't be suicide.

Then his own name came in, and he was missing and was

asked to come forward. And then he read that he was supposed to have gone to London, and he went sick with fear. He went hot and he went cold. Something rose in his throat and choked him. His hands shook as he held the paper; his head whirled with terror.

He was afraid to go home to his room because he knew he could not stay still in it; he would be tramping up and down, like a wild beast, and the landlady would wonder. And he was afraid to be in the streets, for fear a policeman would come behind him and put a hand on his shoulder.

There was a kind of small square round the corner and he sat down on one of the benches there and held up the paper before his face, with the children yelling and howling and playing all about him on the asphalt paths. They took no notice of him, and yet they were company of a sort; it was not like being all alone in that quiet little room. But it soon got dark and the man came to shut the gates.

And after that night: nights and days of horror and sick terrors that he never had known a man could suffer and live.

He had brought enough money to keep him for a while, but every time he changed a note he shook with fear, wondering whether it would be traced. What could he do? Where could he go? Could he get out of the country? But there were passports and papers of all sorts; that would never do.

He read that the police held a clue to the Ledham Murder Mystery; and he trembled to his lodgings and locked himself in and moaned in his agony, and then found himself chattering words and phrases at random, without meaning or relevance; strings of gibbering words: 'all right, all right, all right . . . yes, yes, yes, yes . . . there, there, there . . . well, well, well, well . . . ' just because he could not bear to sit still and silent, with that anguish tearing his heart, with that sick horror choking him, with that weight of terror pressing on his breast.

And then nothing happened; and a little, faint, trembling hope fluttered in his breast for a while, and for a day or two he felt he might have a chance after all.

One night he was in such a happy state that he ventured round to the little pub at the corner, and drank a bottle of Old Brown Ale with some enjoyment, and began to think of what life might be again, if by a miracle – he recognised, even then, that it would be a miracle – all this horror passed away, and he was once more just like other men, with nothing to be afraid of.

He was relishing the Brown Ale, and quite plucking up a spirit, when a chance phrase from the bar caught him: 'Looking for him not far from here, so they say.'

He left the glass of beer half full, and went out wondering whether he had the courage to kill himself that night. As a matter of fact, the men at the bar were talking about a recent and sensational cat burglar; but every such word was doom to this wretch.

And ever and again he would check himself in his horrors, in his mutterings and gibberings, and wonder with amazement that the heart of a man could suffer such bitter agony, such rending torment. It was as if he had found out and discovered – he alone of all men living – a new world of which no man before had ever dreamed, in which no man could believe, if he were told the story of it.

He had awakened in the past from such nightmares, now and again, as most men suffer. They were terrible, so terrible that he remembered two or three of them had oppressed him years before; but they were pure delight to what he now endured. Not endured, but writhed under as a worm twisting amid red, burning coals.

He went out into the streets, some noisy, some dull and empty, and considered in his panic-stricken confusion which he should choose. They were looking for him in that part of London; there was deadly peril in every step. The streets where people went to and fro and laughed and chattered might be the safer; he could walk with the others and seem to be one of them, and so be less likely to be noticed by those who were on his track.

But then, on the other hand, the great electric lamps made these streets almost as bright as day, and every feature of the passers-by was clearly seen. True, he was clean-shaven now, and the pictures of him in the papers showed a bearded man, and his own face in the glass still looked strange to him. Still, there were sharp eyes that could penetrate such disguises; and they might have brought down some man from Ledham who knew him well.

'He was turning aside, making for a very quiet street close by, when he hesitated. This street, indeed, was still enough after dark, and not well lighted. It was a street of low, two-storied houses of grey brick that had grinned with three or four families in each house.

Tired men came home here after working hard all day, and people drew their blinds early and stirred very little abroad, and went early to bed; footsteps were rare in this street and in other streets into which it led, and the lamps were few and dim compared with those in the big thoroughfares.

And yet, the very fact that few people were about made such as were all the more noticeable and conspicuous. And the police went slowly on their beats in the dark streets as in the bright, and with few people to look at, no doubt they looked more keenly at such as passed on the pavement.

In his world, that dreadful world that he had discovered and dwelt in alone, the darkness was brighter than the daylight, and solitude more dangerous than a multitude of men. He dared not go into the light; he feared the shadows, and went trembling to his room and shuddered there as the hours of the night went by; shuddered and gabbled to himself his infernal rosary; 'All right, all right, all right . . . splendid, splendid . . . that's the way, that's the way, that's the way . . . yes, yes, yes . . . first-rate, first-rate – ' gabbled in a low mutter to keep from howling like a wild beast.

It was somewhat in the manner of a wild beast that he beat and tore against the cage of his fate. Now and again it struck him as incredible. He would not believe that it was so. It was something that he would wake from, as he had waked from those nightmares that he remembered, for things did not really happen so. He could not believe it, he would not believe it.

Or, if it were so indeed, then all these horrors must be happening to some other man into whose torments he had mysteriously entered.

Or he had got into a book, into a tale which one read and shuddered at, but did not for one moment credit; all make-believe, it must be, and presumably everything would be all right again. And then the truth came down on him like a heavy hammer, and beat him down.

Now and then he tried to reason with himself. He forced himself to be sensible, as he put it; not to give way, to think of his chances. After all, it was three weeks since he had got into the excursion train at Darnley, and every day of freedom made his chances better.

These things often die down. There were lots of cases in which the police never got the man they were after. He lit his pipe and began to think things over quietly. It might be a good plan to give his landlady notice, and leave at the end of the week, and make for somewhere in South London, and try to get a job of some sort: that would help to put them off his track. He got up and looked thoughtfully out of the window; and caught his breath.

There outside the little newspaper shop opposite, was the bill of the evening paper; New Clue in Ledham Murder Mystery.

The moment came at last. He never knew the exact means by

which he was hunted down. As a matter of fact, a woman who knew him well happened to be standing outside Darnley station on the Excursion Day morning, and she had recognised him, in spite of his beardless chin.

And then, at the other end, his landlady, on her way upstairs, had heard his mutterings and gabblings, though the voice was low. She was interested, and curious, and a little frightened, and wondered if her lodger might be dangerous, and naturally she talked to her friends.

So the story trickled down to the ears of the police, and the police asked about the date of the lodger's arrival. And there you were. And there was our nameless friend, drinking a good, hot cup of tea, and polishing off thè bacon and eggs with rare appetite; in the cosy room with the cheerful paper; otherwise the Condemned Cell.

The Monstrance

So far things were going very well indeed. The night was thick and black and cloudy, and the German force had come three-quarters of their way or more without an alarm. There was no challenge from the English lines; and indeed the English were being kept busy by a high shell-fire on their front. This had been the German plan; and it was coming off admirably. Nobody thought that there was any danger on the left; and so the Prussians, writhing on their stomachs over the ploughed field, were drawing nearer and nearer to the wood. Once there they could establish themselves comfortably and securely during what remained of the night; and at dawn the English left would be hopelessly enfiladed – and there would be another of those movements which people who really understand military matters call 're-adjustments of our line'.

The noise made by the men creeping and crawling over the fields was drowned by the cannonade, from the English side as well as the Germans. On the English centre and right things were indeed very brisk; the big guns were thundering and shrieking and roaring, the machine guns were keeping up the very devil's racket; the flares and illuminating shells were as good as the Crystal Palace in the old days, as the soldiers said to one another. All this had been thought of and thought out on the other side. The German force was beautifully organized. The men who crept nearer and nearer to the wood carried quite a number of machine guns in bits on their backs; others of them had small bags full of sand; yet others big bags that were empty. When the wood was reached the sand from the small bags was to be emptied into the big bags; the machine-gun parts were to be put together, the guns mounted behind the sandbag redoubt, and then, as Major Von und Zu pleasantly observed, 'the English pigs shall to gehenna-fire quickly come.'

The major was so well pleased with the way things had gone that he permitted himself a very low and guttural chuckle; in another ten minutes success would be assured. He half turned his head round to whisper a caution about some detail of the sandbag business to the big sergeant-major, Karl Heinz, who was crawling just behind him. At that instant Karl Heinz leapt into the air with a scream that rent through the night and through all the roaring of the artillery. He cried in a terrible voice, 'The Glory of the Lord!' and plunged and pitched forward, stone dead. They said that his face as he stood up there and cried aloud was as if it had been seen through a sheet of flame.

'They' were one or two out of the few who got back to the German lines. Most of the Prussians stayed in the ploughed field. Karl Heinz's scream had frozen the blood of the English soldiers, but it had also ruined the major's plans. He and his men, caught all unready, clumsy with the burdens that they carried, were shot to pieces; hardly a score of them returned. The rest of the force were attended to by an English burying party. According to custom the dead men were searched before they were buried, and some singular relics of the campaign were found upon them, but nothing so singular as Karl Heinz's diary.

He had been keeping it for some time. It began with entries about bread and sausage and the ordinary incidents of the trenches; here and there Karl wrote about an old grandfather, and a big china pipe, and pinewoods and roast goose. Then the diarist seemed to get fidgety about his health. Thus:

April 17 – Annoyed for some days by murmuring sounds in my head. I trust I shall not become deaf, like my departed uncle Christopher.

April 20 – The noise in my head grows worse; it is a humming sound. It distracts me; twice I have failed to hear the captain and have been reprimanded.

April 22 – So bad is my head that I go to see the doctor. He speaks of *tinnitus*, and gives me an inhaling apparatus that shall reach, he says, the middle ear.

April 25 – The apparatus is of no use. The sound is now become like the booming of a great church bell. It reminds me of the bell at St Lambart on that terrible day of last August.

April 26 – I could swear that it is the bell of St Lambart that I hear all the time. They rang it as the procession came out of the church.

The man's writing, at first firm enough, begins to straggle unevenly over the page at this point. The entries show that he became convinced that he heard the bell of St Lambart's Church ringing, though (as he knew better than most men) there had been no bell and no church at St Lambart's since the summer of 1914. There was no village either – the whole place was a rubbish-heap.

Then the unfortunate Karl Heinz was beset with other troubles.

May 2 – I fear I am becoming ill. To-day Joseph Kleist, who is next to me in the trench, asked me why I jerked my head to the right so constantly. I told him to hold his tongue; but this shows that I am noticed. I keep fancying that there is something white just beyond the range of my sight on the right hand.

May 3 – This whiteness is now quite clear, and in front of me. All this day it has slowly passed before me. I asked Joseph Kleist if he saw a piece of newspaper just beyond the trench. He stared at me solemnly – he is a stupid fool – and said, 'There is no paper.'

May 4 – It looks like a white robe. There was a strong smell of incense to-day in the trench. No one seemed to notice it. There is decidedly a white robe, and I think I can see feet, passing very slowly before me at this moment while I write.

There is no space here for continuous extracts from Karl Heinz's diary. But to condense with severity, it would seem that he slowly gathered about himself a complete set of sensory hallucinations. First the auditory hallucination of the sound of a bell, which the doctor called *tinnitus*. Then a patch of white growing into a white robe, then the smell of incense. At last he lived in two worlds. He saw his trench, and the level before it, and the English lines; he talked with his comrades and obeyed orders, though with a certain difficulty; but he also heard the deep boom of St Lambart's bell, and saw continually advancing towards him a white procession of little children, led by a boy who was swinging a censer. There is one extraordinary entry: 'But in August those children carried no lilies; now they have lilies in their hands. Why should they have lilies?'

It is interesting to note the transition over the border line. After May 2 there is no reference in the diary to bodily illness, with two notable exceptions. Up to and including that date the sergeant knows that he is suffering from illusions; after that he accepts his hallucinations as actualities. The man who cannot see what he sees and hear what he hears is a fool. So he writes: 'I ask who is singing "Ave Maris Stella". That blockhead Friedrich Schumacher raises his crest and answers insolently that no one sings, since singing is strictly forbidden for the present.'

A few days before the disastrous night expedition the last figure in the procession appeared to those sick eyes.

The old priest now comes in his golden robe, the two boys holding each side of it. He is looking just as he did when he died, save that when he walked in St Lambart there was no shining round his head. But this is illusion and contrary to reason, since no one has a shining about his head. I must take some medicine.

Note here that Karl Heinz absolutely accepts the appearance of the martyred priest of St Lambart as actual, while he thinks that the halo must be an illusion; and so he reverts again to his physical condition.

The priest held up both his hands, the diary states, 'as if there were something between them. But there is a sort of cloud or dimness over this object, whatever it may be. My poor Aunt Kathie suffered much from her eyes in her old age.'

One can guess what the priest of St Lambart carried in his hands when he and the little children went out into the hot sunlight to implore mercy, while the great resounding bell of St Lambart boomed over the plain. Karl Heinz knew what happened then; they said that it was he who killed the old priest and helped to crucify the little child against the church door. The baby was only three years old. He died calling piteously for 'mummy' and 'daddy'.

And those who will may guess what Karl Heinz saw when the mist cleared from before the monstrance in the priest's hands. Then he shrieked and died.

THE GIFT OF TONGUES

More than a hundred years ago a simple German maid-of-all-work caused a great sensation. She became subject to seizures of a very singular character, of so singular a character that the family inconvenienced by these attacks were interested and, perhaps a little proud of a servant whose fits were so far removed from the ordinary convulsion. The case was thus. Anna, or Gretchen, or whatever her name might be, would suddenly become oblivious of soup, sausage, and the material world generally.

But she neither screamed, nor foamed, nor fell to earth after the common fashion of such seizures. She stood up, and from her mouth rolled sentence after sentence of splendid sound, in a sonorous tongue, filling her hearers with awe and wonder. Not one of her listeners understood a word of Anna's majestic utterances, and it was useless to question her in her uninspired moments, for the girl knew nothing of what had happened.

At length, as it fell out, some scholarly personage was present during one of these extraordinary fits; and he at once declared that the girl was speaking Hebrew, with a pure accent and perfect intonation. And, in a sense, the wonder was now greater than ever. How could the simple Anna speak Hebrew? She had certainly never learnt it. She could barely read and write her native German. Everyone was amazed, and the occult mind of the day began to formulate theories and to speak of possession and familiar spirits. Unfortunately (as I think, for I am a lover of all insoluble mysteries), the problem of the girl's Hebrew speech was solved; solved, that is, to a certain extent.

The tale got abroad, and so it became known that some years before Anna had been servant to an old scholar. The personage was in the habit of declaiming Hebrew as he walked up and down his study and the passages of his house, and the maid had unconsciously stored the chanted words in some cavern of her soul; in that receptacle, I suppose, which we are content to call the subconsciousness. I must confess that the explanation does not strike me as satisfactory in all respects. In the first place, there is the extraordinary tenacity of memory; but I suppose that other instances of this, though rare enough, might be cited. Then, there is the association of this particular storage of the subconsciousness with a species of seizure; I do not know whether any similar instance can be cited.

Still, minor puzzles apart, the great mystery was mysterious no more: Anna spoke Hebrew because she had heard Hebrew and, in her odd fashion, had remembered it.

To the best of my belief, cases that offer some points of similarity are occasionally noted at the present day. Persons ignorant of Chinese deliver messages in that tongue; the speech of Abyssinia is heard from lips incapable, in ordinary moments, of anything but the pleasing idiom of the United States of America, and untaught Cockneys suddenly become fluent in Basque.

But all this, so far as I am concerned, is little more than rumour; I do not know how far these tales have been subjected to strict and systematic examination. But in any case, they do not interest me so much as a very odd business that happened on the Welsh border more than sixty years ago. I was not very old at the time, but I remember my father and mother talking about the affair, just as I remember them talking about the Franco-Prussian War in the August of 1870, and coming to the conclusion that the French seemed to be getting the worst of it. And later, when I was growing up and the mysteries were beginning to exercise their fascination upon me, I was able to confirm my vague recollections and to add to them a good deal of exact information. The odd business to which I am referring was the so-called 'Speaking with Tongues' at Bryn Sion Chapel, Treowen, Monmouthshire, on a Christmas Day of the early 'seventies.

Treowen is one of a chain of horrible mining villages that wind in and out of the Monmouthshire and Glamorganshire valleys. Above are the great domed heights, quivering with leaves (like the dear Zacynthus of Ulysses), on their lower slopes, and then mounting by far stretches of deep bracken, glittering in the sunlight, to a golden land of gorse, and at last to wild territory, bare and desolate, that seems to surge upward for ever. But beneath, in the valley, are the black pits and the blacker mounds, and heaps of refuse, vomiting chimneys, mean rows and ranks of grey houses faced with red brick; all as dismal and detestable as the eye can see.

Such a place is Treowen; uglier and blacker now than it was sixty years ago; and all the worse for the contrast of its vileness with those glorious and shining heights above it. Down in the town there are three great chapels of the Methodists and Baptists and Congregationalists; architectural monstrosities all three of them, and a red brick church does not do much to beautify the place. But above all this, on the hillside, there are scattered white-washed farms, and a little hamlet of white, thatched cottages, remnants all of a pre-industrial age, and here is situate the old meeting-house called Bryn Sion, which means, I believe, the Brow of Zion. It must have been built about 1790–1800, and, being a simple, square building, devoid of crazy ornament, is quite inoffensive.

Here came the mountain farmers and cottagers, trudging, some of them, long distances on the wild tracks and paths of the hillside; and here ministered, from 1860 to 1880, the Reverend Thomas Beynon, a bachelor, who lived in the little cottage next to the chapel, where a grove of beech-trees was blown into a thin straggle of tossing boughs by the great winds of the mountain.

Now, Christmas Day falling on a Sunday in this year of long ago, the usual service was held at Bryn Sion Chapel, and, the weather being fine, the congregation was a large one—that is, something between forty and fifty people. People met and shook hands and wished each other 'Merry Christmas', and exchanged the news of the week and prices at Newport market, till the elderly, white-bearded minister, in his shining black, went into the chapel. The deacons followed him and took their places in the big pew by the open fireplace, and the little meeting-house was almost full. The minister had a windsor chair, a red hassock, and a pitchpine table in a sort of raised pen at the end of the chapel, and from this place he gave out the opening hymn. Then followed a long portion of Scripture, a second hymn, and the congregation settled themselves to attend to the prayer.

It was at this moment that the service began to vary from the accustomed order. The minister did not kneel down in the usual way; he stood staring at the people, very strangely, as some of them thought. For perhaps a couple of minutes he faced them in dead silence, and here and there people shuffled uneasily in their pews. Then he came down a few paces and stood in front of the table with bowed head, his back to the people. Those nearest to the ministerial pen or rostrum heard a low murmur coming from his lips. They could not make out the words.

Bewilderment fell upon them all, and, as it would seem, a confusion of mind, so that it was difficult afterwards to gather any clear account of what actually happened that Christmas morning at Bryn Sion Chapel. For some while the mass of the congregation heard nothing at all; only the deacons in the Big Seat could make out the swift mutter that issued from their pastor's lips; now a little higher in tone, now sunken so as to be almost inaudible. They strained their ears to discover what he was saying in that low, continued utterance; and they could hear words plainly, but they could not understand. It was not Welsh.

It was neither Welsh—the language of the chapel—nor was it English. They looked at one another, those deacons, old men like their minister most of them; looked at one another with something of strangeness and fear in their eyes. One of them, Evan Tudor, Torymynydd, ventured to rise in his place and to ask the preacher, in a low voice, if he were ill. The Reverend Thomas Beynon took no notice; it was evident that he did not hear the question: swiftly the unknown words passed his lips.

'He is wrestling with the Lord in prayer,' one deacon whispered to another, and the man nodded—and looked frightened.

And it was not only this murmured utterance that bewildered

those who heard it; they, and all who were present, were amazed at the pastor's strange movements. He would stand before the middle of the table and bow his head, and go now to the left of the table, now to the right of it, and then back again to the middle. He would bow down his head, and raise it, and look up, as a man said afterwards, as if he saw the heavens opened. Once or twice he turned round and faced the people, with his arms stretched wide open, and a swift word on his lips, and his eyes staring and seeing nothing, nothing that anyone else could see. And then he would turn again. And all the while the people were dumb and stricken with amazement; they hardly dared to look at each other; they hardly dared to ask themselves what could be happening before them. And then, suddenly, the minister began to sing.

It must be said that the Reverend Thomas Beynon was celebrated all through the valley and beyond it for his 'singing religious eloquence', for that singular chant which the Welsh call the *hwyl*. But his congregation had never heard so noble, so awful a chant as this before. It rang out and soared on high, and fell, to rise again with wonderful modulations; pleading to them and calling them and summoning them; with the old voice of the *hwyl*, and yet with a new voice that they had never heard before: and all in those sonorous words that they could not understand. They stood up in their wonder, their hearts shaken by the chant; and then the voice died away. It was as still as death in the chapel. One of the deacons could see that the minister's lips still moved; but he could hear no sound at all. Then the minister raised up his hands as if he held something between them; and knelt down, and rising, again lifted his hands. And there came the faint tinkle of a bell from the sheep grazing high up on the mountain side.

The Reverend Thomas Beynon seemed to come to himself out of a dream, as they said. He looked about him nervously, perplexed, noted that his people were gazing at him strangely, and then, with a stammering voice, gave out a hymn and afterwards ended the service. He discussed the whole matter with the deacons and heard what they had to tell him. He knew nothing of it himself and had no explanation to offer. He knew no languages, he declared, save Welsh and English. He said that he did not believe there was evil in what had happened, for he felt that he had been in Heaven before the Throne. There was a great talk about it all, and that queer Christmas service became known as the Speaking with Tongues of Bryn Sion.

Years afterwards, I met a fellow-countryman, Edward Williams, in London, and we fell talking, in the manner of exiles, of the land and its stories. Williams was many years older than myself, and he told me of an odd thing that had once happened to him.

'It was years ago,' he said, 'and I had some business—I was a mining-engineer in those days—at Treowen, up in the hills. I had to stay over Christmas, which was on a Sunday that year, and talking to some people there about the *hwyl*, they told me that I ought to go up to Bryn Sion if I wanted to hear it done really well. Well, I went, and it was the queerest service I ever heard of. I don't know much about the Methodists' way of doing things, but before long it struck me that the minister was saying some sort of Mass. I could hear a word or two of the Latin service now and again, and then he sang the Christmas Preface right through: "*Quia per incarnati Verbi mysterium*"—you know.'

Very well; but there is always a loophole by which the reasonable, or comparatively reasonable, may escape. Who is to say that the old preacher had not strayed long before into some Roman Catholic Church at Newport or Cardiff on a Christmas Day, and there heard Mass with exterior horror and interior love?

Strange Occurrence in Clerkenwell

Mr Dyson had inhabited for some years a couple of rooms in a moderately quiet street in Bloomsbury, where, as he somewhat pompously expressed it, he held his finger on the pulse of life without being deafened with the thousand rumours of the main arteries of London. It was to him a source of peculiar, if esoteric, gratification that from the adjacent corner of Tottenham Court Road a hundred lines of omnibuses went to the four quarters of the town; he would dilate on the facilities for visiting Dalston, and dwell on the admirable line that knew extremist Ealing and the streets beyond Whitechapel.

His rooms, which had been originally 'furnished apartments', he had gradually purged of their more peccant parts; and though one would not find here the glowing splendour of his old chambers in the street off the Strand, there was something of severe grace about the appointments which did credit to his taste. The rugs were old, and of the true faded beauty; the etchings, nearly all of them proofs printed by the artist, made a good show with broad white margins and black frames, and there was no spurious black oak.

Indeed there was but little furniture of any kind: a plain and honest table, square and sturdy stood in one corner; a seventeenth-century settle fronted the hearth; and two wooden elbow-chairs and a book-shelf of the Empire made up the equipment, with no exception worthy of note. For Dyson cared for none of these things; his place was at his own bureau, a quaint old piece of lacquered-work, at which he would sit for hour after hour, with his back to the room, engaged in the desperate pursuit of literature, or, as he termed his profession, the chase of the phrase.

The neat array of pigeon-holes and drawers teemed and overflowed with manuscripts and notebooks, the experiments and efforts of many years; and the inner well, a vast and cavernous receptacle, was stuffed with accumulated ideas. Dyson was a craftsman who loved all the detail and the technique of his work intensely; and if, as has been hinted, he deluded himself a little with the name of artist, yet his amusements were eminently harmless, and, so far as

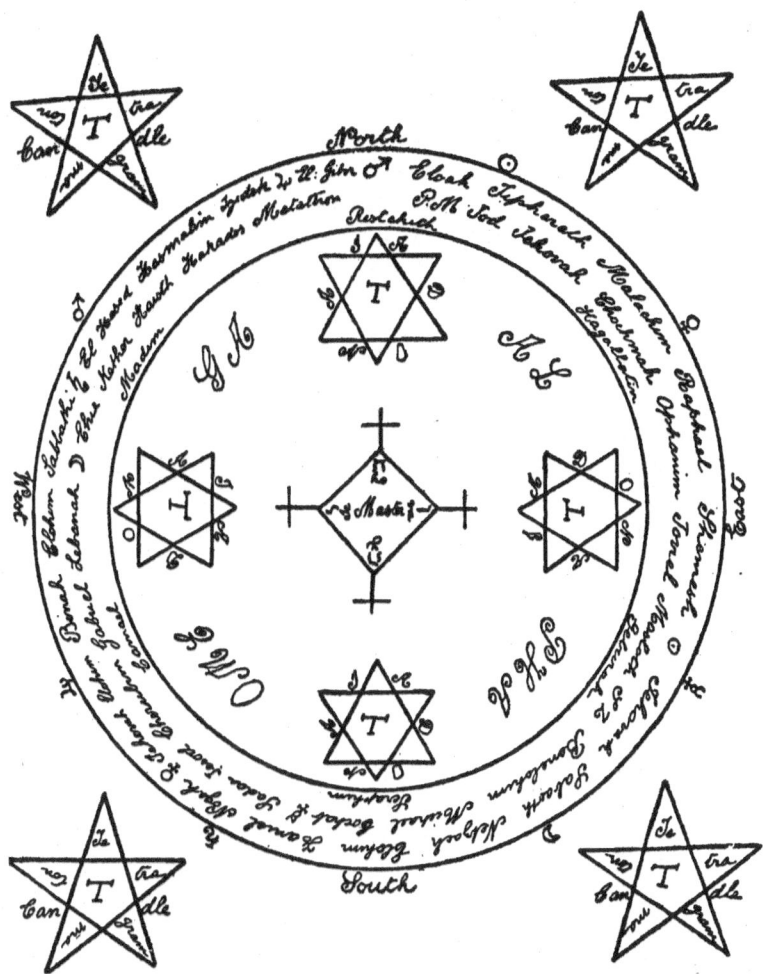

THE MAGICAL CIRCLE

can be ascertained, he (or the publishers) had chosen the good part of not tiring the world with printed matter.

Here, then, Dyson would shut himself up with his fancies, experimenting with words, and striving, as his friend the recluse of Bayswater stove, with the almost invincible problem of style, but always with a fine confidence, extremely different from the chronic depression of the realist. He had been almost continuously at work on some scheme that struck him as well-nigh magical in its possibilities since the night of an adventure with a mysterious tenant from the first floor in Abingdon Grove; and as he laid down the pen with a glow of triumph, he reflected that he had not viewed the streets for five days in succession. With all the enthusiasm of his accomplished labour still working in his brain, he put away his papers and went out, pacing the pavement at first in that rare mood of exultation which finds in every stone upon the way the possibilities of a masterpiece.

It was growing late, and the autumn evening was drawing to a close amidst veils of haze and mist, and in the stilled air the voices, and the roaring traffic, and incessant feet seemed to Dyson like the noise upon the stage when all the house is silent. In the square the leaves rippled down as quick as summer rain, and the street beyond was beginning to flare with the lights in the butchers' shops and the vivid illumination of the greengrocer. It was a Saturday night, and the swarming populations of the slums were turning out in force; the battered women in rusty black had begun to paw the lumps of cagmag, and others gloated over unwholesome cabbages, and there was a brisk demand for four ale.

Dyson passed through these night-fires with some relief; he loved to meditate, but his thoughts were not as De Quincey's after his dose; he cared not two straws whether onions were dear or cheap, and would not have exulted if meat had fallen to two-pence a pound. Absorbed in the wilderness of the tale he had been writing, weighing nicely the points of plot and construction, relishing the recollection of this and that happy phrase, and dreading failure here and there, he left the rush and whistle of the gas-flares behind him, and began to touch upon pavements more deserted.

He had turned, without taking note, to the northward, and was passing through an ancient fallen street, where now notices of floors and offices to let hung out, but still about it lingered the grace and the stiffness of the Age of Wigs – a broad roadway, a broad pavement, and on each side a grave line of houses with long and narrow windows flush with the walls, all of mellowed brickwork. Dyson walked with quick steps, as he resolved that short work must be made of a certain episode; but he was in that happy humour of invention, and another chapter rose in the inner chamber of his brain, and he dwelt on the circumstances he was to write down with curious pleasure.

It was charming to have the quiet streets to walk in, and in his thought he made a whole district the cabinet of his studies, and vowed he would come again. Heedless of his course, he struck off to the east again, and soon found himself involved in a square network of grey two-storied houses, and then in the waste void and elements of brickwork, the passages and unmade roads behind great factory walls, encumbered with the refuse of the neighbourhood, forlorn, ill-lighted, and desperate.

A brief turn, and there rose before him the unexpected, a hill suddenly lifted from the level ground, its steep ascent marked by the lighted lamps, and eager as an explorer, Dyson found his way to the place, wondering where his crooked paths had brought him. Here all was again decorous, but hideous in the extreme. The builder, someone lost in the deep gloom of the early 'twenties, had conceived the idea of twin villas in grey brick, shaped in a manner to recall the outlines of the Parthenon, each with its classic form broadly marked with raised bands of stucco. The name of the street was all strange, and for a further surprise the top of the hill was crowned with an irregular plot of grass and fading trees, called a square, and here again the Parthenon-motive had persisted. Beyond, the streets were curious, wild in their irregularities, here a row of sordid, dingy dwellings, dirty and disreputable in appearance, and there, without warning, stood a house, genteel and prim, with wire blinds and brazen knocker, as clean and trim as if it had been the doctor's house in some benighted little country town. These surprises and discoveries began to exhaust Dyson, and he hailed with delight the blazing windows of a public-house, and went in with the intention of testing the beverage provided for the dwellers in this region, as remote as Libya and Pamphylia and the parts about Mesopotamia.

The babble of voices from within warned him that he was about to assist at the true parliament of the London workman, and he looked about him for that more retired entrance called private. When he had settled himself on an exiguous bench, and had ordered some beer, he began to listen to the jangling talk in the public bar beyond; it was a senseless argument, alternately furious and maudlin, with appeals to Bill and Tom, and mediaeval survivals of speech, words that Chaucer wrote belched out with zeal and relish, and the din of pots jerked down and coppers rapped smartly on the zinc counter made a thorough bass for it all.

Dyson was calmly smoking his pipe between the sips of beer, when an indefinite-looking figure slid rather than walked into the compartment. The man started violently when he saw Dyson placidly sitting in the corner, and glanced keenly about him. He seemed to be on wires, controlled by some electric machine, for he almost bolted out of the door when the barman asked with what he could serve him, and his hand shivered as he took the glass. Dyson inspected him with a little curiosity.

He was muffled up almost to the lips, and a soft felt hat was drawn down over his eyes; he looked as if he shrank from every glance, and a more raucous voice suddenly uplifted in the public bar seemed to find in him a sympathy that made him shake and quiver like a jelly. It was pitiable to see any one so thrilled with nervousness, and Dyson was about to address some trivial remark of casual inquiry to the man, when another person came into the compartment, and, laying his hand on his arm, muttered something in an undertone, and vanished as he came. But Dyson had recognised him as the smooth-tongued and smooth-shaven Burton; and yet he thought little of it, for his whole faculty of observation was absorbed in the lamentable and yet grotesque spectacle before him.

At the first touch of the hand on his arm the unfortunate man had wheeled round as if spun on a pivot, and shrank back with a low, piteous cry, as if some dumb beast were caught in the toils. The blood fled away from the wretch's face, and the skin became grey as if a shadow of death had passed in the air and fallen on it, and Dyson caught a choking whisper –

'Mr Davies! For God's sake, have pity on me, Mr Davies! On my oath, I say –' and his voice sank to silence as he heard the message, and strove in vain to bite his lips, and summon up to his aid some tinge of manhood. He stood there a moment, wavering as the leaves of an aspen, and then he was gone out into the street, as Dyson thought silently, with his doom upon his head. He had not been gone a minute when it suddenly flashed into Dyson's mind that he knew the man; it was undoubtedly the young man with spectacles for whom so many ingenious persons were searching; the spectacles indeed were missing, but the pale face, the dark whiskers, and the timid glances were enough to identify him.

Dyson saw at once that by a succession of hazards he had unawares hit upon the scent of some desperate conspiracy, wavering as the track of a loathsome snake in and out of the highways and byways of the London cosmos; the truth was instantly pictured before him, and he divined that all unconscious and unheeding he had been privileged to see the shadows of hidden forms, chasing and hurrying, and grasping and vanishing across the bright curtain of common life, soundless and silent, or only babbling fables and pretences.

For him in an instant the jargoning of voices, the garish splendour, and all the vulgar tumult of the public-house became part of magic; for here before his eyes a scene in this grim mystery play had been enacted, and he had seen human flesh grow cold with a palsy of fear; the very hell of cowardice and terror had gaped wide within an arm's breadth. In the midst of these reflections the barman came up and stared at him as if to hint that he had exhausted his right to take his ease, and Dyson bought another lease of the seat by an order for more beer. As he pondered the brief glimpse of tragedy, he recollected that with his first start of haunted fear the young man with whiskers had drawn his hand swiftly from his greatcoat pocket, and that he had heard something fall to the ground; and pretending to have dropped his pipe, Dyson began to grope in the corner, searching with his fingers. He touched something and drew it gently to him, and with one brief glance, as he put it quietly in his pocket, he saw it was a little old-fashioned notebook, bound in faded green morocco.

He drank down his beer at a gulp, and left the place, overjoyed at his fortunate discovery, and busy with conjecture as to the possible importance of the find. By turns he dreaded to find perhaps mere blank leaves, or the laboured follies of a betting-book, but the faded morocco cover seemed to promise better things, and to hint at mysteries. He piloted himself with no little difficulty out of the sour and squalid quarter he had entered with a light heart, and emerging at Gray's Inn Road, struck off down Guilford Street and hastened home, only anxious for a lighted candle and solitude.

Dyson sat down at his bureau, and placed the little book before him; it was an effort to open the leaves and dare disappointment. But in desperation at last he laid his fingers between the pages at haphazard, and rejoiced to see a compact range of writing with a margin, and as it chanced, three words caught his glance and stood out apart from the mass. Dyson read –

'*the Gold Tiberius*'

and his face flushed with fortune and the lust of the hunter.

He turned at once to the first leaf of the pocket-book, and proceeded to read with rapt interest the

HISTORY OF THE YOUNG MAN WITH SPECTACLES

From the filthy and obscure lodgings, situated, I verily believe, in one of the foulest slums of Clerkenwell, I indite this history of a life which, daily threatened, cannot last very much longer. Every day – nay, every hour, I know too well my enemies are drawing their nets closer about me; even now I am condemned to be a close prisoner in my squalid room, and I know that when I go out I shall go to my destruction. This history, if it chance to fall into good hands, may, perhaps, be of service in warning young men of the dangers and pitfalls that most surely must accompany any deviation from the ways of rectitude.

My name is Joseph Walters. When I came of age I found myself in possession of a small but sufficient income, and I determined that I would devote my life to scholarship. I do not mean the scholarship of these days; I had no intention of associating myself with men whose lives are spent in the unspeakably degrading occupation of 'editing' classics, befouling the fair margins of the fairest books with idle and superfluous annotation, and doing their utmost to give a lasting disgust of all that is beautiful. An abbey church turned to the base use of a stable or bakehouse is a sorry sight; but more pitiable still is a masterpiece spluttered over with the commentator's pen, and his hideous mark 'cf.'.

For my part, I chose the glorious career of scholar in its ancient sense; I longed to possess encyclopaedic learning, to grow old amongst books, to distil day by day, and year after year, the inmost sweetness of all worthy writings. I was not rich enough to collect a library, and I was therefore forced to betake myself to the reading-room of the British Museum.

O dim, far-lifted, and mighty dome, Mecca of many minds, mausoleum of many hopes, sad house where all desires fail! For there men enter in with hearts uplifted, and dreaming minds, seeing in those exalted stairs a ladder to fame, in that pompous portico the gate of knowledge, and going in, find but vain vanity, and all but in vain. There, when the long streets are ringing, is silence, there eternal twilight, and the odour of heaviness. But there the blood flows thin and cold, and the brain burns adust; there is the hunt of shadows, and the chase of embattled phantoms, a striving against ghosts and a war that has no victory. O dome, tomb of the quick! surely in thy galleries, where no reverberant voice can call, sighs whisper ever, and mutterings of dead hopes; and there men's souls mount like moths towards the flame, and fall scorched and blackened beneath thee, O dim, far-lifted, and mighty dome!

Bitterly do I now regret the day when I took my place at a desk for the first time, and began my studies. I had not been an habitué of the place for many months, when I became acquainted with a serene and benevolent gentleman, a man somewhat past middle age, who nearly always occupied a desk next to mine. In the reading-room it takes little to make an acquaintance – a casual offer of assistance, a hint as to the search in the catalogue, and the ordinary politeness of men who constantly sit near each other; it was thus I came to know the man calling himself Dr Lipsius. By degrees I grew to look for his presence, and to miss him when he was away, as was sometimes the case, and so a friendship sprang up between us. His immense range of learning was placed freely at my service; he would often astonish me by the way in which he would sketch out in a few minutes the bibliography of a given subject, and before long I had confided to him my ambitions.

'Ah,' he said, 'you should have been a German. I was like that myself when I was a boy. It is a wonderful resolve, an infinite career. I will know all things; yes, it is a device indeed. But it means this – a life of labour without end, and a desire unsatisfied at last. The scholar has to die, and die saying, "I know very little!" '

Gradually, by speeches such as these, Lipsius seduced me : he would praise the career, and at the same time hint that it was as hopeless as the search for the philosopher's stone, and so by artful suggestions, insinuated with infinite address, by degrees he succeeded in undermining all my principles. 'After all,' he used to say, 'the greatest of all sciences, the key to all knowledge, is the science and art of pleasure. Rabelais was perhaps the greatest of all the encyclopaedic scholars; and he, as you know, wrote the most remarkable book that has ever been written. And what does he teach men in this book? Surely the joy of living.

'I need not remind you of the words, suppressed in most of the editions, the key of all the Rabelaisian mythology, of all the enigmas of his grand philosophy, *Vivez joyeux*. There you have all his learning; his work is the institutes of pleasure as the fine art; the finest art there is : the art of all arts. Rabelais had all science, but he had all life too. And we have gone a long way since his time. You are enlightened, I think; you do not consider all the petty rules and by-laws that a corrupt society has made for its own selfish convenience as the immutable decrees of the Eternal.'

Such were the doctrines that he preached; and it was by such insidious arguments, line upon line, here a little and there a little, that he at last succeeded in making me a man at war with the whole social system. I used to long for some opportunity to break the chains and to live a free life, to be my own rule and measure. I viewed existence with the eyes of a pagan, and Lipsius understood to perfection the art of stimulating the natural inclinations of a young man hitherto a hermit. As I gazed up at the great dome I saw it flushed with the flames and colours of a world of enticement unknown to me, my imagination played me a thousand wanton tricks, and the forbidden drew me as surely as a loadstone draws on iron. At last my resolution was taken, and I boldly asked Lipsius to be my guide.

He told me to leave the Museum at my usual hour, half past four, to walk slowly along the northern pavement of Great Russell Street, and to wait at the corner of the street till I was addressed, and then to obey in all things the instructions of the person who came up to me. I carried out these directions, and stood at the corner looking about me anxiously, my heart beating fast, and my breath coming in gasps. I waited there for some time, and had begun to fear I had been made the object of a joke, when I suddenly became conscious of a gentleman who was looking at me with evident amusement from the opposite pavement of Tottenham Court Road. He came over and, raising his hat, politely begged me to follow him, and I did so without a word wondering where we were going, and what was to happen.

I was taken to a house of quiet and respectable aspect in a street lying to the north of Oxford Street, and my guide rang a bell. A servant showed us into a large room quietly furnished, on the ground floor. We sat there in silence for some time, and I noticed that the furniture, though unpretending, was extremely valuable. There were large oak presses, two book-cases of extreme elegance, and in one corner a carved chest which must have been mediaeval.

Presently, Dr Lipsius came in and welcomed me with his usual manner, and after some desultory conversation my guide left the room. Then an elderly man dropped in, and began talking to Lipsius, and from their conversation I understood that my friend was a dealer in antiques; they spoke of the Hittite seal, and of the prospects of further discoveries, and later, when two or three more persons joined us, there was an argument as to the possibility of a systematic exploration of the pre-Celtic monuments in England. I was, in fact, present at an archaeological reception of an informal kind, and at nine o'clock, when the antiquaries were gone, I stared at Lipsius in a manner that showed I was puzzled, and sought an explanation.

'Now,' he said, 'we will go upstairs.'

As we passed up the stairs, Lipsius lighting the way with a hand-lamp, I heard the sound of a jarring lock and bolts and bars shot on at the front door. My guide drew back a baize door and we went down a passage, and I began to hear odd sounds, a noise of curious mirth; then he pushed me through a second door, and my initiation began. I cannot write down what I witnessed that night; I cannot bear to recall what went on in those secret rooms fast shuttered and curtained so that no light should escape into the quiet street; they gave me red wine to drink, and a woman told me as I sipped it that it was wine of the Red Jar that Avallaunius had made. Another asked me how I liked the wine of the Fauns, and I heard a dozen fantastic names, while the stuff boiled in my veins, and stirred, I think, something that had slept within me from the moment I was born.

It seemed as if my self-consciousness deserted me; I was no

longer a thinking agent, but at once subject and object; I mingled in the horrible sport, and watched the mystery of the Greek groves and fountains enacted before me, saw the reeling dance and heard the music calling as I sat beside my mate, and yet I was outside it all, and viewed my own part an idle spectator. Thus with strange rites they made me drink the cup, and when I woke up in the morning I was one of them, and had sworn to be faithful.

At first I was shown the enticing side of things; I was bidden to enjoy myself and care for nothing but pleasure, and Lipsius himself indicated to me as the acutest enjoyment the spectacle of the terrors of the unfortunate persons who were from time to time decoyed into the evil house. But after a time it was pointed out to me that I must take my share in the work, and so I found myself compelled to be in my turn a seducer; and thus it is on my conscience that I have helped many to the depths of the pit.

One day Lipsius summoned me to his private room, and told me that he had a difficult task to give me. He unlocked a drawer and gave me a sheet of typewritten paper, and bade me read it.

It was without place, or date, or signature, and ran as follows:

Mr James Headley, F.S.A., will receive from his agent in Armenia, on the 12th inst., a unique coin, the gold Tiberius. It bears on the reverse a faun with the legend *Victoria*. It is believed that this coin is of immense value. Mr Headley will come up to town to show the coin to his friend, Professor Memys, of Chenies Street, Oxford Street, on some date between the 13th and the 18th.

Dr Lipsius chuckled at my face of blank surprise when I laid down this singular communication.

'You will have a good chance of showing your discretion,' he said. 'This is not a common case; it requires great management and infinite tact. I am sure I wish I had a Panurge in my service, but we will see what you can do.'

'But is it not a joke?' I asked him. 'How can you know – or rather, how can this correspondent of yours know – that a coin has been despatched from Armenia to Mr Headley? And how is it possible to fix the period in which Mr Headley will take it into his brain to come up to town? It seems to me a lot of guesswork.'

'My dear Mr Walters,' he replied, 'we do not deal in guesswork here. It would bore you if I went into all these little details, the cogs and wheels, if I may say so, which move the machine. Don't you think it is much more amusing to sit in front of the house and be astonished than to be behind the scenes and see the mechanics? Better tremble at the thunder, believe me, than see the man rolling the cannon-ball. But, after all, you needn't bother about the how and why; you have your share to do. Of course I shall give you full instructions, but a great deal depends on the way the thing is carried out. I have often heard very young men maintain that style is everything in literature, and I can assure you that the same maxim holds good in our far more delicate profession. With us style is absolutely everything, and that is why we have friends like yourself.'

I went away in some perturbation : he had no doubt designedly left everything in mystery, and I did not know what part I should have to play. Though I had assisted at scenes of hideous revelry, I was not yet dead to all echo of human feeling, and I trembled lest I should receive the order to be Mr Headley's executioner.

A week later, it was on the sixteenth of the month, Dr Lipsius made me a sign to come into his room.

'It is for tonight,' he began. 'Please to attend carefully to what I am going to say, Mr Walters, and on peril of your life, for it is a dangerous matter – on peril of your life, I say, follow these instructions to the letter. You understand? Well, tonight at about half past seven, you will stroll quietly up the Hampstead Road till you come to Vincent Street. Turn down here and walk along, taking the third turning to your right, which is Lambert Terrace. Then follow the terrace, cross the road, and go along Hertford Street, and so into Lillington Square. The second turning you will come to in the Square is called Sheen Street; but in reality it is more a passage between blank walls than a street.

'Whatever you do, take care to be at the corner of this street at eight o'clock precisely. You will walk along it, and just at the bend where you lose sight of the square you will find an old gentleman with white beard and whiskers. He will in all probability be abusing a cabman for having brought him to Sheen Street instead of Chenies Street. You will go up to him quietly and offer your services; he will tell you where he wants to go, and you will be so courteous as to offer to show him the way. I may say that Professor Memys moved into Chenies Street a month ago; thus Mr Headley has never been to see him there, and, moreover, he is very short-sighted, and knows little of the topography of London. Indeed, he has quite lived the life of a learned hermit at Audley Hall.

'Well, need I say more to a man of your intelligence? You will bring him to this house, he will ring the bell, and a servant in quiet livery will let him in. Then your work will be done, and I am sure done well. You will leave Mr Headley at the door, and simply continue your walk, and I shall hope to see you the next day. I really don't think there is anything more I can tell you.'

These minute instructions I took care to carry out to the letter. I confess that I walked up the Tottenham Court Road by no means blindly, but with an uneasy sense that I was coming to a decisive point in my life. The noise and rumour of the crowded pavements were to me but dumb show; I revolved again and again in ceaseless iteration the task that had been laid on me, and I questioned myself as to the possible results. As I got near the point of turning, I asked myself whether danger were not about my steps; the cold thought struck me that I was suspected and observed, and every chance foot-passenger who gave me a second glance seemed to me an officer of police. My time was running out, the sky had darkened, and I hesitated, half resolved to go no farther but to abandon Lipsius and his friends forever. I had almost determined to take this course, when the conviction suddenly came to me that the whole thing was a gigantic joke, a fabrication of rank improbability. Who could have procured the information about the Armenian agent? I asked myself. By what means could Lipsius have known the particular day and the very train that Mr Headley was to take? How engage him to enter one special cab amongst the dozens waiting at Paddington?

I vowed it a mere Milesian tale, and went forward merrily, turned down Vincent Street, and threaded out the route that Lipsius had so carefully impressed upon me. The various streets he had named were all places of silence and an oppressive cheap gentility; it was dark, and I felt alone in the musty squares and crescents, where people pattered by at intervals, and the shadows were growing blacker.

I entered Sheen Street, and found it as Lipsius had said, more a passage than a street; it was a byway, on one side a low wall and neglected gardens, and grim backs of a line of houses, and on the other a timber-yard. I turned the corner, and lost sight of the square, and then, to my astonishment, I saw the scene of which I had been told. A hansom cab had come to a stop beside the pavement, and an old man, carrying a handbag, was fiercely abusing the cabman, who sat on his perch the image of bewilderment.

'Yes, but I'm sure you said Sheen Street, and that's where I brought you,' I heard him saying as I came up, and the old gentleman boiled in a fury, and threatened police and suits at law.

The sight gave me a shock, and in an instant I resolved to go through with it. I strolled on, and without noticing the cabman, lifted my hat politely to old Mr Headley.

'Pardon me, sir,' I said, 'but is there any difficulty? I see you are a traveller; perhaps the cabman has made a mistake. Can I direct you?'

The old fellow turned to me, and I noticed that he snarled and showed his teeth like an ill-tempered cur as he spoke.

'This drunken fool has brought me here,' he said. 'I told him to drive to Chenies Street, and he brings me to this infernal place. I won't pay him a farthing, and I meant to have given him a handsome sum. I am going to call for the police and give him in charge.'

At this threat the cabman seemed to take alarm; he glanced around, as if to make sure that no policeman was in sight, and drove off grumbling loudly, and Mr Headley grinned savagely with satisfaction at having saved his fare, and put back one and sixpence into his pocket, the 'handsome sum' the cabman had lost.

'My dear sir,' I said, 'I am afraid this piece of stupidity has annoyed you a great deal. It is a long way to Chenies Street, and you will have some difficulty in finding the place unless you know London pretty well.'

'I know it very little,' he replied. 'I never come up except on important business, and I've never been to Chenies Street in my life.'

'Really? I should be happy to show you the way. I have been for a stroll, and it will not at all inconvenience me to take you to your destination.'

'I want to go to Professor Memys, at No. 15. It's most annoying to me; I'm short-sighted, and I can never make out the numbers on the doors.'

'This way if you please,' I said, and we set out.

I did not find Mr Headley an agreeable man; indeed, he grumbled the whole way. He informed me of his name, and I took care to say, 'The well-known antiquary?' and thenceforth I was compelled to listen to the history of his complicated squabbles with publishers, who treated him, as he said, disgracefully; the man was a chapter in the Irritability of Authors. He told me that he had been on the point of making the fortune of several firms, but had been compelled to abandon the design owing to their rank ingratitude.

Besides these ancient histories of wrong, and the more recent misadventure of the cabman, he had another grievous complaint to make. As he came along in the train, he had been sharpening a pencil, and the sudden jolt of the engine as it drew up at a station had driven the penknife against his face, inflicting a small triangular wound just on the cheekbone, which he showed me. He denounced the railway company, heaped imprecations on the head of the driver, and talked of claiming damages. Thus he grumbled all the way, not noticing in the least where he was going; and so unamiable did his conduct seem to me, that I began to enjoy the trick I was playing on him.

Nevertheless, my heart beat a little faster as we turned into the street where Lipsius was waiting. A thousand accidents, I thought, might happen; some chance might bring one of Headley's friends to meet us; perhaps, though he knew not Chenies Street, he might know the street where I was taking him; in spite of his short sight, he might possibly make out the number, or, in a sudden fit of suspicion, he might make an enquiry of the policeman at the corner. Thus every step upon the pavement, as we drew nearer to the goal, was to me a pang and a terror, and every approaching passenger carried a certain threat of danger. I gulped down my excitement with an effort, and made shift to say pretty quietly –

'No. 15, I think you said? That is the third house from this. If you will allow me, I will leave you now; I have been delayed a little, and my way lies on the other side of Tottenham Court Road.'

He snarled out some kind of thanks, and I turned my back and walked swiftly in the opposite direction. A minute or two later I looked round and saw Mr Headley standing on the doorstep, and then the door opened and he went in. For my part, I gave a sigh of relief; I hastened to get away from the neighbourhood, and endeavoured to enjoy myself in merry company.

The whole of the next day I kept away from Lipsius. I felt anxious, but I did not know what had happened, or what was happening, and a reasonable regard for my own safety told me that I should do well to remain quietly at home. My curiosity, however, to learn the end of the odd drama in which I had played a part stung me to the quick, and late in the evening I made up my mind to see how events had turned out. Lipsius nodded when I came in, and asked if I could give him five minutes' talk. We went to his room, and he began to walk up and down, while I sat waiting for him to speak.

'My dear Mr Walters,' he said at length, 'I congratulate you warmly; your work was done in the most thorough and artistic manner. You will go far. Look.'

He went to his *escritoire* and pressed a secret spring; a drawer flew out, and he laid something on the table. It was a gold coin! I took it up and examined it eagerly, and read the legend about the figure of the faun.

'Victoria,' I said, smiling.

'Yes; it was a great capture, which we owe to you. I had great difficulty in persuading Mr Headley that a little mistake had been made, that was how I put it. He was very disagreeable, and indeed ungentlemanly, about it; didn't he strike you as a very cross old man?'

I held the coin, admiring the choice and rare design, clear cut as if from the mint; and I thought the fine gold glowed and burnt like a lamp.

'And what finally became of Mr Headley?' I said at last.

Lipsius smiled and shrugged.

'What on earth does it matter?' he said. 'He might be here, or there, or anywhere; but what possible consequence could it be? Besides, your question rather surprises me; you are an intelligent man, Mr Walters. Just think it over, and I'm sure you won't repeat the question.'

'My dear sir,' I said, 'I hardly think you are treating me fairly. You have paid me some handsome compliments on my share in the capture, and I naturally wish to know how the matter ended. From what I saw of Mr Headley I should think you must have had some difficulty with him.'

He gave me no answer for the moment, but began again to walk up and down the room, apparently absorbed in thought.

'Well,' he said at last, 'I suppose there is something in what you say. We are certainly indebted to you. I have said that I have a high opinion of your intelligence, Mr Walters. Just look here, will you?'

He opened a door communicating with another room, and pointed.

There was a great box lying on the floor, a queer, coffin-shaped thing. I looked at it, and saw it was a mummy case, like those in the British Museum, vividly painted in the brilliant Egyptian colours, with I knew not what proclamation of dignity or hopes of life immortal. The mummy swathed about in the robes of death was lying within, and the face had been uncovered.

'You are going to send this away?' I said, forgetting the question I had put.

'Yes; I have an order from a local museum. Look a little more closely.'

Puzzled by his manner, I peered into the face, while he held the lamp. The flesh was black with the passing of the centuries; but as I looked I saw upon the right cheek bone a small triangular scar, and the secret of the mummy flashed upon me : I was looking at the dead body of the man whom I had decoyed into that house.

There was no thought or design of action in my mind. I held the accursed coin in my hand, burning me with a foretaste of hell, and I fled as I would have fled from pestilence and death, and dashed into the street in blind horror, not knowing where I went. I felt the gold coin grasped in my clenched fist, and throwing it away, I knew not where, I ran on and on through by-streets and dark ways, till at last I issued out into a crowded thoroughfare and checked myself. Then as consciousness returned I realised my instant peril, and understood what would happen if I fell into the hands of Lipsius. I knew that I had put forth my finger to thwart a relentless mechanism rather than a man.

My recent adventure with the unfortunate Mr Headley had taught me that Lipsius had agents in all quarters; and I foresaw that if I fell into his hands, he would remain true to his doctrine of style, and cause me to die a death of some horrible and ingenious torture. I bent my whole mind to the task of outwitting him and his emissaries, three of whom I knew to have proved their ability for tracking down persons who for various reasons preferred to remain obscure. These servants of Lipsius were two men and a woman, and the woman was incomparably the most subtle and the most deadly. Yet I considered that I too had some portion of craft, and I took my resolve. Since then I have matched myself day by day against the ingenuity of Lipsius and his myrmidons.

For a time I was successful; though they beat furiously after me in the covert of London, I remained *perdu*, and watched with some amusement their frantic efforts to recover the scent lost in two or three minutes. Every lure and wile was put forth to entice me from my hiding-place; I was informed by the medium of the public prints that what I had taken had been recovered, and meetings were proposed in which I might hope to gain a great deal without the slightest risk. I laughed at their endeavours, and began a little to despise the organisation I had so dreaded, and ventured more abroad. Not once or twice, but several times, I recognised the two men who were charged with my capture, and I succeeded in eluding them at close quarters; and a little too hastily I decided that I had nothing to dread, and that my craft was greater than theirs.

But in the meanwhile, while I congratulated myself on my cunning, the third of Lipsius's emissaries was weaving her nets; and in an evil hour I paid a visit to an old friend, a literary man named Russell, who lived in a quiet street in Bayswater. The woman, as I found out too late, a day or two ago occupied rooms in the same house, and I was followed and tracked down. Too late, as I have said, I recognised that I had made a fatal mistake, and that I was besieged.

Sooner or later I shall find myself in the power of an enemy without pity; and so surely as I leave this house I shall go to receive doom. I hardly dare to guess how it will at last fall upon me; my imagination, always a vivid one, paints to me appalling pictures of the unspeakable torture which I shall probably endure; and I know that I shall die with Lipsius standing near and gloating over the refinements of my suffering and my shame.

Hours, nay minutes, have become precious to me. I sometimes pause in the midst of anticipating my tortures, to wonder whether even now I cannot hit upon some supreme stroke, some design of infinite subtlety, to free myself from the toils. But I find that the faculty of combination has left me; I am as the scholar of the old myth, deserted by the power which has helped me hitherto. I do not know when the supreme moment will come, but sooner or later, it is inevitable; before long I shall receive sentence, and from the sentence to execution will not be long. . . .

*

I cannot remain here a prisoner any longer. I shall go out tonight when the streets are full of crowds and clamours, and make a last effort to escape. . . .

*

It was with profound astonishment that Dyson closed the little book, and thought of the strange series of incidents which had brought him into touch with the plots and counterplots connected with the Gold Tiberius. He had bestowed the coin carefully away, and he shuddered at the bare possibility of its place of deposit becoming known to the evil band who seemed to possess such extraordinary sources of information.

It had grown late while he read, and he put the pocket-book away, hoping with all his heart that the unhappy Walters might even at the eleventh hour escape the doom he dreaded.

'A wonderful story, as you say, an extraordinary sequence and play of coincidence. I confess that your expressions when you first showed me the Gold Tiberius were not exaggerated. But do you think that Walters has really some fearful fate to dread?'

'I cannot say. Who can presume to predict events when life itself puts on the robe of coincidence and plays at drama? Perhaps we have not yet reached the last chapter in the queer story. But, look, we are drawing near to the verge of London; there are gaps, you see, in the serried ranks of brick, and a vision of green fields beyond.'

Dyson had persuaded the ingenious Mr Phillipps to accompany him on one of those aimless walks to which he was himself so addicted. Starting from the very heart of London, they had made their way westward through the stony avenues, and were now just emerging from the red lines of an extreme suburb, and presently the half-finished road ended, a quiet land began, and they were beneath the shade of elm trees. The yellow autumn sunlight that had lit up the bare distance of the suburban street now filtered down through the boughs of the trees and shone on the glowing carpet of fallen leaves, and the pools of rain glittered and shot back the gleam of light. Over all the broad pastures there was peace and the happy rest of autumn before the great winds begin, and afar off London lay all vague and immense amidst the veiling mist; here and there a distant window catching the sun and kindling with fire, and a spire gleaming high, and below the streets in shadow, and the turmoil of life. Dyson and Phillipps walked on in silence beneath the high hedges, till at a turn of the lane they saw a mouldering and ancient gate standing open, and the prospect of a house at the end of a moss-grown carriage drive.

'There is a survival for you,' said Dyson; 'it has come to its last days, I imagine. Look how the laurels have grown gaunt and weedy, and black and bare beneath; look at the house, covered with yellow wash, and patched with green damp. Why, the very notice-board, which informs all and singular that the place is to be let, has cracked and half fallen.'

'Suppose we go in and see it,' said Phillipps; 'I don't think there is anybody about.'

They turned up the drive, and walked slowly towards this remnant of old days. It was a large, straggling house, with curved wings at either end, and behind a series of irregular roofs and projections, showing that the place had been added to at divers dates; the two wings were roofed in cupola fashion, and at one side, as they came nearer, they could see a stableyard, and a clock turret with a bell, and the dark masses of gloomy cedars. Amidst all the lineaments of dissolution there was but one note of contrast : the sun was setting beyond the elm trees, and all the west and south were in flames; on the upper windows of the house the glow shone reflected, and it seemed as if blood and fire were mingled. Before the yellow front of the mansion, stained, as Dyson had remarked, with gangrenous patches, green and blackening, stretched what had once been, no doubt, a well-kept lawn, but it was now rough and ragged, and nettles and great docks, and all manner of coarse weeds, struggled in the places of the flower-beds.

The urns had fallen from their pillars beside the walk, and lay broken in shards upon the ground, and everywhere from grass-plot and path a fungoid growth had sprung up and multiplied, and lay dank and slimy like a festering sore upon the earth. In the middle of the rank grass of the lawn was a desolate fountain; the rim of the basin was crumbling and pulverised with decay, and within the water stood stagnant, with green scum for the lilies that had once bloomed there; rust had eaten into the bronze flesh of the Triton that stood in the middle, and the conch-shell he held was broken.

'Here,' said Dyson, 'one might moralise over decay and death. Here all the stage is decked out with the symbols of dissolution; the cedarn gloom and twilight hang heavy around us, and everywhere within the pale darkness has found a harbour, and the very air is changed and brought to accord with the scene. To me, I confess, this deserted house is as moral as a graveyard, and I find something sublime in that lonely Triton, deserted in the midst of his water-pool. He is the last of the gods; they have left him, and he remembers the sound of water falling on water, and the days that were sweet.'

'I like your reflections extremely,' said Phillipps; 'but I may mention that the door of the house is open.'

'Let us go in, then.'

The door was just ajar, and they passed into the mouldy hall and looked in at a room on one side. It was a large room, going far back, and the rich, old, red flock paper was peeling from the walls in long strips, and blackened with vague patches of rising damp; the ancient clay, the dank reeking earth rising up again, and subduing all the work of men's hands after the conquest of many years. The floor was thick with the dust of decay, and the painted ceiling fading from all gay colours and light fancies of cupids in a career, and disfigured with sores of dampness, seemed transmuted into other work.

No longer the amorini chased one another pleasantly, with limbs that sought not to advance and hands that merely simulated the act of grasping at the wreathed flowers; but it appeared some savage burlesque of the old careless world and of its cherished conventions, and the dance of the Lovers had become a Dance of Death; black pustules and festering sores swelled and clustered on fair limbs and smiling faces showed corruption, and the fairy blood had boiled with the germs of foul disease; it was a parable of the leaven working, and worms devouring for a banquet the heart of a rose.

Strangely, under the painted ceiling, against the decaying walls, two old chairs still stood alone, the sole furniture of the empty place. High-backed, with curving arms and twisted legs, covered with faded gold leaf, and upholstered in tattered damask, they too were a part of the symbolism, and struck Dyson with surprise. 'What have we here?' he said. 'Who has sat in these chairs? Who, clad in peach-blossom satin, with lace ruffles and diamond buckles, all golden, *a conté fleurettes* to his companion? Phillipps, we are in another age. I wish I had some snuff to offer you, but failing that I beg to offer you a seat, and we will sit and smoke.'

They sat down on the queer old chairs, and looked out of the dim and grimy panes to the ruined lawn, and the fallen urns, and the deserted Triton.

'It's a foolish fancy,' Dyson said then; 'but I keep thinking I hear a noise like some one groaning. Listen; no, I can't hear it now. There it is again! Did you notice it, Phillipps?'

'No, I can't say I heard anything. But I believe that old places like this are like shells from the shore, ever echoing with noises. The old beams, mouldering piecemeal, yield a little and groan; and such a house as this I can fancy all resonant at night with voices, the voices of matter so slowly and so surely transformed into other shapes, the voice of the worm that gnaws at last the very heart of the oak, the voice of stone grinding on stone, and the voice of the conquest of Time.'

They sat still in the old arm-chairs, and grew graver in the musty ancient air.

'I don't like the place,' said Phillipps, after a long pause. 'To me it seems as if there were a sickly, unwholesome smell about it, a smell of something burning.'

'You are right; there is an evil odour here. Hark! Did you hear that?'

A hollow sound, a noise of infinite sadness and infinite pain, broke in upon the silence, and the two men looked fearfully at one another, horror, and the sense of unknown things, glimmering in their eyes.

'Come,' said Dyson, 'we must see into this,' and they went into the hall.

'Do you know,' said Phillipps, 'it seems absurd, but I could almost fancy that the smell is that of burning flesh.'

They went up the hollow-sounding stairs, and the odour became thick and noisome, stifling the breath, and a vapour, sickening as the smell of the chamber of death, choked them. A door was open, and they entered the large upper room, and clung hard to one another, shuddering at the sight they saw.

A naked man was lying on the floor, his arms and legs stretched wide apart, and bound to pegs that had been hammered into the boards. The body was torn and mutilated in the most hideous fashion, scarred with the marks of red-hot irons, a shameful ruin of the human shape. But upon the middle of the body a fire of coals was smouldering; the flesh had been burnt through. The man was dead, but the smoke of his torment mounted still, a black vapour.

'The young man with spectacles,' said Mr Dyson.

THE BOWMEN

It was during the Retreat of the Eighty Thousand, and the authority of the Censorship is sufficient excuse for not being more explicit. But it was on the most awful day of that awful time, on the day when ruin and disaster came so near that their shadow fell over London far away; and, without any certain news, the hearts of men failed within them and grew faint; as if the agony of the army in the battlefield had entered into their souls.

On this dreadful day, then, when three hundred thousand men in arms with all their artillery swelled like a flood against the little English company, there was one point above all other points in our battle line that was for a time in awful danger, not merely of defeat, but of utter annihilation. With the permission of the Censorship and of the military expert, this corner may, perhaps, be described as a salient, and if this angle were crushed and broken, then the English force as a whole would be shattered, the Allied left would be turned, and Sedan would inevitably follow.

All the morning the German guns had thundered and shrieked against this corner, and against the thousand or so of men who held it. The men joked at the shells, and found funny names for them, and had bets about them, and greeted them with scraps of music-hall songs. But the shells came on and burst, and tore good Englishmen limb from limb, and tore brother from brother, and as the heat of the day increased so did the fury of that terrific cannonade. There was no help, it seemed. The English artillery was good, but there was not nearly enough of it; it was being steadily battered into scrap iron.

There comes a moment in a storm at sea when people say to one another, "It is at its worst; it can blow no harder," and then there is a blast ten times more fierce than any before it. So it was in these British trenches.

There were no stouter hearts in the whole world than the hearts of these men; but even they were appalled as this seven-times-heated hell of the German cannonade fell upon them and overwhelmed them and destroyed them. And at this very moment they saw from their trenches that a tremendous host was moving against their lines. Five hundred of the thousand remained, and as far as they could see the German infantry was pressing on against them, column upon column, a grey world of men, ten thousand of them, as it appeared afterwards.

There was no hope at all. They shook hands, some of them. One man improvised a new version of the battle-song, "Good-bye, good-bye to Tipperary," ending with "And we shan't get there." And they all went on firing steadily. The officers pointed out that such an opportunity for high-class, fancy shooting might never occur again; the Germans dropped line after line; the Tipperary humorist asked, "What price Sidney Street?" And the few machine guns did their best. But everybody knew it was of no use. The dead grey bodies lay in companies and battalions, as others came on and on and on, and they swarmed and stirred and advanced from beyond and beyond.

"World without end. Amen," said one of the British soldiers with some irrelevance as he took aim and fired. And then he remembered – he says he cannot think why or wherefore – a queer vegetarian restaurant in London where he had once or twice eaten eccentric dishes of cutlets made of lentils and nuts that pretended to be steak. On all the plates in this restaurant there was printed a figure of St George in blue, with the motto, *Adsit Anglis Sanctus Georgius* – May St George be a present help to the English. This soldier happened to know Latin and other useless things, and now, as he fired at his man in the grey advancing mass – 300 yards away – he uttered the pious vegetarian motto. He went on firing to the end, and at last Bill on his right had to clout him cheerfully over the head to make him stop, pointing out as he did so that the King's ammunition cost money and was not lightly to be wasted in drilling funny patterns into dead Germans.

For as the Latin scholar uttered his invocation he felt something between a shudder and an electric shock pass through his body. The roar of the battle died down in his ears to a gentle murmur; instead of it, he says, he heard a great voice and a shout louder than a thunder-peal crying, "Array, array, array!"

His heart grew hot as a burning coal, it grew cold as ice within him, as it seemed to him that a tumult of voices answered to his summons. He heard, or seemed to hear, thousands shouting: "St George! St George!"

"Ha! messire; ha! sweet Saint, grant us good deliverance!"

"St George for merry England!"

"Harow! Harow! Monseigneur St George, succour us."

"Ha! St George! Ha! St George! a long bow and a strong bow."

"Heaven's Knight, aid us!"

And as the soldier heard these voices he saw before him, beyond the trench, a long line of shapes, with a shining about them. They were like men who drew the bow, and with another shout their cloud of arrows flew singing and tingling through the air towards the German hosts.

The other men in the trench were firing all the while. They had no hope; but they aimed just as if they had been shooting at Bisley.

Suddenly one of them lifted up his voice in the plainest English.

"Gawd help us!" he bellowed to the man next to him, "but we're blooming marvels! Look at those grey . . . gentlemen, look at them! D'ye see them? They're not going down in dozens, nor in 'undreds; it's thousands, it is. Look! look! there's a regiment gone while I'm talking to ye."

"Shut it!" the other soldier bellowed, taking aim, "what are ye gassing about?"

But he gulped with astonishment even as he spoke, for, indeed, the grey men were falling by the thousands. The English could hear the guttural scream of the German officers, the crackle of their revolvers as they shot the reluctant; and still line after line crashed to the earth.

All the while the Latin-bred soldier heard the cry:

"Harow! Harow! Monseigneur, dear saint, quick to our aid! St George help us!"

"High Chevalier, defend us!"

The singing arrows fled so swift and thick that they darkened the air; the heathen horde melted from before them.

"More machine guns!" Bill yelled to Tom.

"Don't hear them," Tom yelled back. "But, thank God, anyway; they've got it in the neck."

In fact, there were ten thousand dead German soldiers left before that salient of the English army, and consequently there was no Sedan. In Germany, a country ruled by scientific principles, the Great General Staff decided that the contemptible English must have employed shells containing an unknown gas of a poisonous nature, as no wounds were discernible on the bodies of the dead German soldiers. But the man who knew what nuts tasted like when they called themselves steak knew also that St George had brought his Agincourt Bowmen to help the English.

The soldier's rest

The soldier with the ugly wound in the head opened his eyes at last, and looked about him with an air of pleasant satisfaction.

He still felt drowsy and dazed with some fierce experience through which he had passed, but so far he could not recollect much about it. But an agreeable glow began to steal about his heart – such a glow as comes to people who have been in a tight place and have come through it better than they had expected. In its mildest form this set of emotions may be observed in passengers who have crossed the Channel on a windy day without being sick. They triumph a little internally, and are suffused with vague, kindly feelings.

The wounded soldier was somewhat of this disposition as he opened his eyes, pulled himself together, and looked about him. He felt a sense of delicious ease and repose in bones that had been racked and weary, and deep in the heart that had so lately been tormented there was an assurance of comfort – of the battle won. The thundering, roaring waves were passed; he had entered into the haven of calm waters. After fatigues and terrors that as yet he could not recollect he seemed now to be resting in the easiest of all easy chairs in a dim, low room.

In the hearth there was a glint of fire and a blue, sweet-scented puff of wood smoke; a great black oak beam roughly hewn crossed the ceiling. Through the leaded panes of the windows he saw a rich glow of sunlight, green lawns, and against the deepest and most radiant of all blue skies the wonderful far-lifted towers of a vast Gothic cathedral – mystic, rich with imagery.

'Good Lord!' he murmured to himself. 'I didn't know they had such places in France. It's just like Wells. And it might be the other day when I was going past the Swan, just as it might be past that window, and asked the ostler what time it was, and he says, "What time? Why, summer-time"; and there outside it looks like summer that would last for ever. If this was an inn they ought to call it "The Soldiers' Rest".'

He dozed off again, and when he opened his eyes once more a kindly looking man in some sort of black robe was standing by him.

'It's all right now, isn't it?' he said, speaking in good English.

'Yes, thank you, sir, as right as can be. I hope to be back again soon.'

'Well, well; but how did you come here? Where did you get

that?' he pointed to the wound on the soldier's forehead. The soldier put his hand up to his brow and looked dazed and puzzled.

'Well, sir,' he said at last. 'It was like this, to begin at the beginning. You know how we came over in August, and there we were in the thick of it, as you might say, in a day or two. An awful time it was, and I don't know how I got through it alive. My best friend was killed dead beside me as we lay in the trenches. By Cambrai, I think it was.

'Then things got a little quieter for a bit, and I was quartered in a village for the best part of a week. She was a very nice lady where I was, and she treated me proper with the best of everything. Her husband he was fighting; but she had the nicest little boy I ever knew, a little fellow of five, or six it might be, and we got on splendid. The amount of their lingo that kid taught me – "We, we" and "Bong swor" and "Commong voo porty voo", and all – and I taught him English. You should have heard that nipper say "'Arf a mo', old un'!" It was a treat.

'Then one day we got surprised. There was about a dozen of us in the village, and two or three hundred Germans came down on us early one morning. They got us; no help for it. Before we could shoot.

'Well, there we were. They tied our hands behind our backs, and smacked our faces and kicked us a bit, and we were lined up opposite the house where I'd been staying.

'And then that poor little chap broke away from his mother, and he run out and saw one of the Boshes, as we call them, fetch me one over the jaw with his clenched fist. Oh dear! oh dear! he might have done it a dozen times if only that little child hadn't seen him.

'He had a poor bit of a toy I'd bought him at the village shop; a toy gun it was. And out he came running, as I say, crying out something in French like "Bad man! bad man! don't hurt my Anglish or I shoot you"; and he pointed that gun at the

German soldier. The German, he took his bayonet, and he drove it right through the poor little chap's throat.'

The soldier's face worked and twitched and twisted itself into a sort of grin, and he sat grinding his teeth and staring at the man in the black robe. He was silent for a little. And then he found his voice, and the oaths rolled terrible, thundering from him, as he cursed that murderous wretch, and bade him go down and burn for ever in hell. And the tears were raining down his face, and they choked him at last.

'I beg your pardon, sir, I'm sure,' he said, 'especially you being a minister of some kind, I suppose; but I can't help it. He was such a dear little man.'

The man in black murmured something to himself: '*Pretiosa in conspectu Domini mors innocentium ejus*' – Dear in the sight of the Lord is the death of His innocents. Then he put a kind hand very gently on the soldier's shoulder.

'Never mind,' said he; 'I've seen some service in my time, myself. But what about that wound?'

'Oh, that; that's nothing. But I'll tell you how I got it. It was just like this. The Germans had us fair, as I tell you, and they shuts us up in a barn in the village; just flung us on the ground and left us to starve seemingly. They barred up the big door of the barn, and put a sentry there, and thought we were all right.

'There were sort of slits like very narrow windows in one of the walls, and on the second day it was, I was looking out of these slits down the street, and I could see those German devils were up to mischief. They were planting their machine guns everywhere handy where an ordinary man coming up the street would never see them, but I see them, and I see the infantry lining up behind the garden walls. Then I had a sort of a notion of what was coming; and presently, sure enough, I could hear some of our chaps singing "Hullo, hullo, hullo!" in the distance; and I says to myself, "Not this time."

'So I looked about me, and I found a hole under the wall; a kind of a drain I should think it was, and I found I could just squeeze through. And I got out and crept round, and away I goes running down the street, yelling for all I was worth, just as our chaps were getting round the corner at the bottom. "Bang, bang!" went the guns, behind me and in front of me, and on each side of me, and then – bash! something hit me on the head and over I went; and I don't remember anything more till I woke up here just now.'

The soldier lay back in his chair and closed his eyes for a moment. When he opened them he saw that there were other people in the room beside the minister in the black robes. One was a man in a big black cloak. He had a grim old face and a great beaky nose. He shook the soldier by the hand.

'By God! sir,' he said, 'you're a credit to the British Army; you're a damned fine soldier and a good man, and, by God! I'm proud to shake hands with you.'

And then someone came out of the shadow, someone in queer clothes such as the soldier had seen worn by the heralds when he had been on duty at the opening of Parliament by the King.

'Now, by Corpus Domini,' this man said, 'of all knights ye be noblest and gentlest, and ye be of fairest report, and now ye be a brother of the noblest brotherhood that ever was since this world's beginning, since ye have yielded dear life for your friends' sake.'

The soldier did not understand what the man was saying to him. There were others, too, in strange dresses, who came and spoke to him. Some spoke in what sounded like French. He could not make it out; but he knew that they all spoke kindly and praised him.

'What does it all mean?' he said to the minister. 'What are they talking about? They don't think I'd let down my pals?'

'Drink this,' said the minister, and he handed the soldier a great silver cup, brimming with wine.

The soldier took a deep draught, and in that moment all his sorrows passed from him.

'What is it?' he asked.

'*Vin nouveau du Royaume*,' said the minister. 'New Wine of the Kingdom, you call it.' And then he bent down and murmured in the soldier's ear.

'What,' said the wounded man, 'the place they used to tell us about in Sunday School? With such drink and such joy—'

His voice was hushed. For as he looked at the minister the fashion of his vesture was changed. The black robe seemed to melt away from him. He was all in armour, if armour be made of starlight, of the rose of dawn, and of sunset fires; and he lifted up a great sword of flame.

Full in the midst, his Cross of Red
Triumphant Michael brandished,
And trampled the Apostate's pride.

ARTHUR MACHEN

Arthur Machen was born in Caerleon, Monmouthshire, Wales in 1863. At the age of eleven, he boarded at Hereford Cathedral School, where he received a comprehensive classical education. Family poverty ruled out going to university, and Machen was sent to London, where he sat entrance exams at medical school but failed to get in. In the capital, he lived in relative poverty, working in a variety of short-lived jobs and exploring the city during the evenings. However, he began to show literary promise; in 1881, at the age of just eighteen, he published a long poem, 'Eleusinia', and in 1884, he published his second work, the pastiche *The Anatomy of Tobacco*.

By 1890, Machen was publishing in literary magazines, and writing stories with Gothic and fantastic themes. His first major success came in 1894, with the novella *The Great God Pan*. Although widely denounced by the press as degenerate and horrific because of its decadent style and sexual content, it has since garnered a reputation as a classic of horror; indeed, author Stephen King has called it "maybe the best [horror story] in the English language."

Machen next produced *The Three Impostors* (1895), a novel composed of a number of interwoven tales which are now regarded as some of his best works.

Between 1900 and 1910, Machen dabbled in acting, and published what is generally seen as his *magnum opus, The Hill of Dreams* (1907). He accepted a full-time journalist's job at Alfred Harmsworth's *Evening News* in 1910, where he remained throughout the war, not leaving until 1921. Machen accepted this role mainly to pay his bills – fiction-writing was his true passion, and he carried on producing novels and short stories throughout the 1910s – but he came to be regarded as a great Fleet Street character by his contemporaries.

The early 1920s saw something of a Machen boom; his works became popular in America, and he brought out his two-volume autobiography. However, by 1929 he was struggling financially again, and left London with his family. It was only a literary appeal launched on the occasion of his eightieth birthday – which drew contributions from admirers such as T. S. Eliot and Bernard Shaw – that eventually ended Machen's money woes. He died some years later in Beaconsfield, Buckinghamshire, England, aged 84.

His legacy remains formidable; his work has influenced countless other artists, and is seen as setting the stage for – amongst other things – the Cthulhu horrors of H. P. Lovecraft.

www.ingramcontent.com/pod-product-compliance
Lightning Source LLC
Chambersburg PA
CBHW051249180626
46816CB00004BA/1398